THIS DINOSAUR ACTIVITY BOOK BELONGS TO:

....

Samantha
Meredith

Kasia
Nowowiejska

DINO BABIES

Tippy-tap! The eggs are cracking. But, oh dear me . . .
One little dino's on his own. Where can his mummy be?

Match the mummy dinosaur stickers to their eggs.

Can you spot
1 beetle?

HAPPY HERDS

The dinosaurs are on the move. Boom-baboom they go!
"Have you seen my mummy?" Baby T-rex wants to know.

Have you seen my mummy?

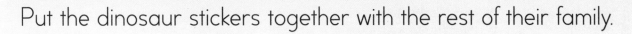

Put the dinosaur stickers together with the rest of their family.

Can you find
2 trees
and 3 eggs?

FAMILY FOOTPRINTS

These footprints might lead Baby T-rex to his mum and dad.
His friends can help him look for them. And that will make him glad.

Can you see
4 ants and 5 birds?

Match the dinosaurs with their footprints.

HIDE 'N' SEEK

Some dinosaurs have patterns that are great for hide 'n' seek.
Is Mummy T-rex one of them? Let's go and take a peek.

Put the dinosaurs in
their best hiding places.

Can you spot
6 caterpillars
and 7 dragonflies?

HIGH IN THE SKY

Flying high, up in the sky, the pterosaurs love soaring.
But Baby T-rex has a question: "Where's my mum?" he's roaring.

Put the pterosaurs in the sky and the treetops.

Can you spot 8 pine cones?

Where's my mum?

ON THE RUN

Look! That volcano's blowing up. Rumble! Crash-bang-boom!
But is that loud noise something else? We're sure to find out soon . . .

ROAAAR!

Help the dinosaurs run away from the noise.

Can you count
9 rocks?

   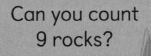 

HAPPY FAMILIES

It's Mummy T-rex! She's been searching for her son all day.
At last the family's back together. Hip-hip-hip-hooray!

Put all your T-rex stickers together in one happy herd.

Can you spot 10 earwigs?

DOT TO DOT

Join the dots to find out who is stomping in the sunshine.

DINO BABIES

HAPPY HERDS

FAMILY FOOTPRINTS

Baby
T-rex

HIDE 'N' SEEK

Baby
T-rex

HIGH IN THE SKY

Baby T-rex

ON THE RUN

HAPPY FAMILIES

Baby
T-rex

WHOSE FOOTPRINTS?

BOOM! BOOM! BOOM! A great big dinosaur just passed by, but who was it? Match the fooprints to find the answer.

A

B

C

D

STEG EGGS!

Lead Mummy Stegosaurus through the maze to reach her eggs before they all hatch!

COLOURING IN

Colour in this picture of Baby Diplodocus hatching from her egg.

GUESS WHO?

Circle the picture of the dinosaur that this shadow belongs to.

PRETTY AS A PICTURE

Colour in this scene using the five colours next to the numbers below.

1 2 3 4 5

MISSING PIECE

Circle the jigsaw piece that completes the picture.

DRAW THE DINO

Can you copy this picture of a triceratops?
Use the grid to help you, and colour
her in when you are finished.

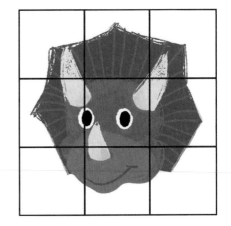

FINISH ME OFF

This T-rex is missing a few important bits! Can you draw in the gaps?

HEADS AND TAILS

These dinosaurs have got all mixed up. Can you help? Draw a line between the heads and tails to match them back up.

IN A TANGLE

Where are these dinosaurs going?
Follow the trails with your finger to find out!

DINO DILEMMA

These diplodocus babies all look the same,
and their mummy can't tell them apart.
Can you help by decorating them?

DINOSAUR DANCE!

These stegosaurus and triceratops babies have got jumbled up. Can you count how many there are of each?

HOW MANY STEGOSAURUS?_____

HOW MANY TRICERATOPS?_____

WHO AM I?

Read the clues below to work out which animal is being described.

A **B** **C**

I have four legs

I have spikes along my back

I have a very long neck

WHO AM I? _____

RACE TIME

These velociraptors all think they're the fastest, but who will reach the volcano first? The trail with the fewest footprints will be the winner!

DINOSAUR DREAMING

This guanlong is dreaming about going on holiday.
Can you draw where he'd like to go?

PREHISTORIC PARTY

This plesiosaur is waiting for his friends.
Can you draw three dinosaurs he'd like to play with?

ODD ONE OUT!

These dinosaurs seem identical, but one is different to the others. Can you find him?

DECORATE A DINOSAUR!

Many dinosaurs had feathers or brightly coloured patterns.
Can you colour in these dinosaurs?

FLYING HIGH

Purple Pterosaur and her friends are swooping through the skies!
Can you count them?

HOW MANY? _____

TWO BY TWO

These dinosaurs are each part of a pair.
Can you match them up?

WHERE'S MY MUMMY?

This baby diplodocus has lost his mummy!
Can you help him through the maze to find her?

DINO BABIES

HAPPY HERDS

FAMILY FOOTPRINTS

HIDE 'N' SEEK

HIGH IN THE SKY

ON THE RUN

HAPPY FAMILIES

P16 **DOT TO DOT**

P17 **WHOSE FOOTPRINTS?**

P18 **STEG EGGS!**

P20 **GUESS WHO?**

P28 **DINOSAUR DANCE**

There are 7 stegosaurus

and 7 triceratops on the page.

P21 **PRETTY AS A PICTURE**

P29 **WHO AM I?**

P33 **ODD ONE OUT!**

P30 **RACE TIME**

P22 **MISSING PIECE**

P24 **FINISH ME OFF**

P35 **FLYING HIGH**

There are 7 pterosaurs flying on the page.

P25 **HEADS AND TAILS**

P26 **IN A TANGLE**

P36 **TWO BY TWO**

P37 **WHERE'S MY MUMMY?**

COLLECT THEM ALL!

Little Snappers sticker books are perfect for
busy hands and curious minds. With lots to spot on every page,
they are packed full of entertaining activities and fun stickers –
guaranteed to get imaginations running wild!

DINOSAURS

FARMYARD

IN THE JUNGLE

UNDER THE SEA

CATERPILLAR BOOKS
An imprint of the Little Tiger Group • www.littletiger.co.uk
1 Coda Studios, 189 Munster Road, London SW6 6AW
First published in Great Britain 2015
Text by Stephanie Stansbie
Text copyright © Caterpillar Books 2015
Scene illustrations copyright © Samantha Meredith 2015
Character illustrations copyright © Kasia Nowowiejska 2015
All rights reserved • Printed in China
ISBN: 978-1-84869-159-9 • CPB/1800/0945/0718
2 4 6 8 10 9 7 5 3